PHILIP WOODERSON
Arf and the
Happy Campers

Arf is now older and (a little) wiser and
ready to embark on his first hilarious
full-length adventure!

Arf expects to have to stay at home
during the school holidays, while his
sisters enjoy a trip to France. However, the
plans go awry and he finds himself running
a camping ground and re-enacting
a battle between the Saxons
and the Normans!

First published 2004 by
A & C Black Publishers Ltd
37 Soho Square, London, W1D 3QZ

www.acblack.com

Text copyright © 2004 Philip Wooderson
Illustrations copyright © 2004 Bridget MacKeith

ISBN 0-7136-6856-3

A CIP catalogue for this book is available from the British Library.

A&C Black uses paper produced with elemental chlorine-free
pulp, harvested from managed sustained forests.

Printed and bound in Spain by G. Z. Printek, Bilbao.

PHILIP WOODERSON

Arf and the Happy Campers

Illustrated by Bridget MacKeith

A & C Black • London

For Meow and Giraffe

Chapter One

It was just typical.

There was one thing Arf wanted to do, and was he allowed to do it? NO. Instead, he would have to do the last thing he wanted to do. Could anyone say that was fair, when it was the start of the summer hols – the best time of the year, so called – and he had to stay at home and NOT go camping in France?

He was telling Mum this in the kitchen, while she was clearing up lunch. 'Gloria and Bee get to go, Mum, and they don't love camping the way I do!'

'You've never been camping,' said Gloria, Arf's elder sister.

'That's why I want to try it,' cried Arf. 'And in any case, neither have you. You told Bee it's going to be yucky having to sleep in a tent and use the public toilets. You said people only do it because it saves them money.'

'I never said that!'

'Yes, she did, Mum. I heard her say the Gullivers couldn't afford a hotel.'

'Don't talk like that, Arf, it's not nice' said Mum.

'But I never said it.' Arf cried.

'I heard you!'

'He's always lying,' said Gloria, 'and making things up! He's so horrid!'

'Oh both of you, sssssh,' said Mum, tired of their constant arguing.

She hadn't had the cash to take them on holiday this year, thanks to the boiler packing up and the front of the house needing painting. So she had been relieved when the Gullivers had offered to take the girls to France. Gloria and Bee were friends with their girls, after all, but Arf felt unfairly left out.

'I've been discriminated against!' he said.

'Oh no you haven't,' said Mum. 'And you and I can have fun while they're gone. We've got the town festival!'

Groan. Arf knew that Mr Gulliver had been its chief organiser and even he wasn't staying. He claimed he had made a mistake with the dates for his holiday. Arf was sure he had done it on purpose.

'I like Mr Gulliver, Mum,' said Arf. 'That's why I'd still like to go camping.'

'He doesn't like you,' put in Gloria. 'Or else he'd have offered to take you too. But he knew you'd be a nuisance to everyone else, so it's your fault.'

'Ignore her,' said Mum.

And he did too. Arf walked across to the window, telling himself some people did not deserve a reply. In the garden he could see Bee, his younger sister. She was trying to put up her tent. 'Hey, what's Bee doing that here for? She hasn't even got to France yet!'

'She's practising, nitwit,' said Gloria.

'Looks like she needs to,' said Arf. 'I'd better go out and help her.'

'Just leave her alone, Arf,' said Mum.

'It's my garden too!'

'Yes, of course, but ...' Mum gave an enormous sigh. 'The girls will be gone in a couple of hours and then you can do what you like. Until then, it might be better for us to keep out of their way, so—'

Arf knew by Mum's tone of voice that she was going to say something drastic, even before she said it.

'Let's go to the supermarket!'

Arf hated the supermarket. At least, he hated the bits where his mum spent most of her time, filling up bags with fruit and veg, and choosing the best sort of loo roll.

He let out another great groan. Could life get worse than this?

* * *

When they got to the supermarket Mum sent him off on a mission to pick up the breakfast cereals.

Frosties or Cocopops? Arf took one of each, forgetting to get the cornflakes that Mum had put on the list. Then he tried to take a quick detour to pick up some packets of crisps, by way of the chocolate biscuits, only to find the aisle was blocked by a fat man pushing a trolley.

His paunch was so huge it had popped the middle buttons on his tight blue shirt and was bulging out over his shorts. His legs were white and hairless. On his head he had black curly hair. He looked like an overgrown kid, except for his droopy moustache. But the weirdest thing was, Arf noticed, there was a boy with the man, a boy a bit older than Arf, and the boy looked just like his dad. Fat, with black hair, in tight shorts, with podgy white legs and trainers (but without a moustache – as yet).

Bad luck, thought Arf, to have such a Dad *and* end up looking just like him! But what on earth were they up to?

They had been loading their trolley with nothing but bottles of wine. And it was all one sort of wine, called Kanga Creek. Three for the price of two. Thirty for twenty, more likely or – actually – sixty for forty! Arf wondered if they did their shopping like this for chips and loo paper too? A trolley of each, so they'd need a big truck to drive all their shopping away! Not surprising the dad was so hefty!

Then the boy stuck his tongue out at Arf. He did it slowly and sourly, as if he couldn't care less.

OK, so Arf might have been staring but, 'No need to be rude ...' said Arf.

Then the boy shoved the trolley straight at him. The trolley was so overloaded that one of the bottles fell out. Arf did his best to catch it but it slipped right out of his hands. It smashed and wine splashed everywhere, all over Arf's trainers and jeans.

'Oy, look what you've done,' Arf protested.

But the boy and his dad scooted off down the aisle, leaving Arf by himself as a man in a white shop coat hurried across, looking very angry.

Then Mum appeared out of nowhere. 'Oh Arf, what have you done?'

'No, Mum, it was those two over there.' He looked round, but where had they disappeared to?

'You can't wriggle out of it, son' said the man. 'You'll have to pay for that bottle–'

'Hey, no, that's not fair.'

'Yes, it is,' said Mum.

'I didn't do it, I promise!'

'But that's what you always say, Arf!'

'And it's always true when I say it!'

Mum sighed. 'I should never have brought you. I just thought you'd help, for a change! But maybe it's best if you go to the park and leave me to finish the shopping. I'll pay and you can settle up later, out of your pocket money.'

* * *

Arf pushed off to the park, amazed Mum had made the suggestion. She hadn't even warned him about not trampling on the flowerbeds. He supposed she had just wanted him out of the way.

How was he going to manage, having to pay for

that bottle? He was already badly in debt, thanks to a stupid bet he had lost with Gloria, over the tennis. He couldn't tell Mum about that, though – betting was banned in their house.

Then Arf caught sight of one of his friends standing outside the park gate. He suggested they kick a ball round.

'Like to, but can't,' said Ricko.

'Why not?'

'The festival, Arf.'

The park was crowded with people, unloading things from cars and vans, and banging nails into posts, hanging up flags on lines and setting out tables and chairs. Most of the stalls were for boring things like potted plants and vegetables, with monster marrows and carrots and wishy watercolours of pets and views by boring local artists.

Ricko said his older brother was working on one of the stalls. 'It's like a bowling alley and people will have to buy tickets. It's going to make loads of money.'

That sounded more like it. 'Let's help,' suggested Arf.

'They can't keep the money,' said Ricko. 'It's just to raise funds for something. Oh yeah, for the fencing club.'

Arf belonged to the fencing club. He had persuaded Mum to pay for fencing lessons. He was learning how to parry and thrust so he could fight duals with swords. He had to wear a mask and thick white protective clothing.

It took them a while to make their way from the gate to the fencing club stall. The stall had canvas walls on both sides and the fencers were emptying sacks of sand on to the ground inside it. Ricko's brother, Steve, was there. Everyone at the club called him 'Slash' because he was junior champion. He was strapping a couple of dummies that looked like Guy Fawkes and Mrs Fawkes on to a couple of poles. The poles had been banged in the ground near the wooden wall at the far end.

'Hi, Slash!' called Arf, 'What are you doing?'

'What does it look like?' said Slash, putting a hat on each dummy. Then he picked a coconut covered in thick brown hair. 'One each on top of their heads – you win if you knock a nut off.'

'What do you win?'

'What d'you think?' Slash bonked the nut on Arf's head.

'But what if you don't like coconuts?'

Slash shrugged. 'That's just too bad. We can't waste money on prizes.'

Arf saw the logic in this. 'Except that only the people who want to eat coconuts are going to waste money on tickets.'

'They'll do it for fun,' said Ricko.

'In that case, why not make it more fun?' said Arf.

'Like how?'

Arf had an idea. He whispered in Slash's ear. 'Dress one in a suit with a spotty bow tie and the other can have pointy specs and a wig.'

Slash looked at him blankly. 'Why?'

Before he had time to explain, two heads popped over the top of the wooden wall at the end. The headteacher and Ms Vespy.

The HT was wearing his usual suit and spotted bow tie. Ms Vespy was twitching her pointy nose so her pointy specs twitched too, jostling her straight black hair. Ms Vespy taught them French. She liked having spelling tests and giving people detentions.

Slash turned to Arf with a look of grudging respect. But instead of thanking him, Slash hastily changed the subject, as if he was jealous of Arf for having such a great idea. He said 'I'm selling my table football game, if you want to buy it?'

'I'd love to', said Arf. 'There's just one small snag.' It was actually quite a big snag. 'I'll have to find some money.'

15

Chapter Two

Arf walked home feeling more cheerful. This festival might be fun after all if he helped on the coconut shy. The club should make pots of money, all thanks to his clever idea.

But then Arf remembered the fact that he needed pots of money himself, to make up for that broken bottle and pay off his other debts, and now to get that table football. He had wanted a table football for yonks, but how could he raise the cash?

He reckoned it would have been only fair if Mum paid him compensation for missing his holiday. But life *wasn't* fair; never had been. As their next-door neighbour, Bill Bott, had once said, 'You just have to do what you can, and make the best of things, Arfie.'

But how was he meant to do that? He needed to look on the bright side. At least his sisters would soon be gone. Then the garden would be all his. And then …

Arf thought of something.

OK, so he couldn't go to France, but he could

still have his own camp, if he rigged up a tent on the grass. He might even get some friends round to stay. They could light a fire and cook some burgers.

But then he had a better idea – a very much better idea.

Yes, this was an even better idea than improving the coconut shy!

If he was to open a campsite why shouldn't he advertise it and bring in other campers, and get them to pay to stay?

He was still wondering about this when he bumped into Bee. She was cradling their little dog, Hoppa, and neither of them looked happy.

'Hoppa's going to be lonely,' she said. 'Mum will be out every day, helping down at the park. You will take care of him, won't you?'

'He can come on my campsite' said Arf.

'You're not going camping,' said Bee.

'Never said that I was *going* camping …'

He told her the first part of his idea to make the garden a campsite, so people would come and stay. 'Then Hoppa can be like my guard dog, and bark and give me warning if campers try and slip off before they've paid their bill.'

The trouble was, Gloria heard this.

'Who'd pay to come *here*?' she demanded.

Arf swung round. 'Hey, don't listen in!'

'She's right, though,' said Bee. 'I don't think it would work. This place is too boring for holidays.'

'Why?' Arf turned back to Bee. 'I bet you, that's what the French people say about France – except they'd say it in French – "I can't think who'd want to come here!"'

'You do, stupid!' cried Gloria.

'I don't any more,' said Arf. 'I'd rather stay on my own campsite. What's so different about where you're going?'

Gloria shrieked with laughter. 'Nothing – except there's a sandy beach and we can swim in the sea. And the sun's going to shine all the time, and there will be lovely French food.'

'And pony trekking,' said Bee.

Arf managed to shrug all this off. 'Bet they don't have a festival week!'

'You told Mum the festival's boring,' said Bee.

'So what? I've changed my mind, now I'm running the coconut shy! It's going to make pots of money. I've had a fantastic idea.'

'Not another one' said Gloria. 'Go on then, try and impress us.'

But Arf was saved from this by Mum calling from the house to say that the girls should come and get ready. 'The Gullivers will be here soon. They won't want to hang about. You've all got a ferry to catch!'

So Arf was left by himself.

He couldn't set up his campsite until the girls had gone. So now there was nothing to do and this was very frustrating. He spent a bit of time pacing round the garden. He thought of Slash with his rapier. He could do with a good fencing fight!

Hurrying up to his bedroom he got out his sword and his mask and sneaked back down to the garden and started to practise his thrusts. But his parries and thrusts seemed a right waste of time without an opponent to go for. He had to close his eyes and imagine a phantom enemy charging out (like Ms Vespy) attacking him with a sharp dagger. He jumped back and forth. He plunged with his blade and the apple tree got in the way, so he went for it, scoring a kill!

But as he stood back, and lifted his mask, expecting to see Ms Vespy lying there, flat on her back, he heard people clapping and cheering.

Oh, drat it. Not only his sisters, but their two friends, Sammy and Sue. They had all come out in the garden intending to say good-bye.

'That tree put up a good fight,' called their dad.

Jim Gulliver was a big shambling man with a boyish fringe of fair hair. He was wearing a long-sleeved shirt rolled up over the elbows, baggy trousers and and hefty brown sandals over thick white socks. He suddenly grabbed the yard broom.

'Okay, Arf, a proper duel?'

'No.' The Number One Rule at the club was not to fight an untrained swordsman. It was too easy to kill them.

But Jim came at Arf with a blood-curdling yell, swinging the broom back and forth, so Arf had to parry him promptly. And then again, and another one too. Arf was soon in retreat down the garden.

It wasn't a very long garden. Arf needed to strike back and quickly (this was just self-defence), but Jim did not not fight by the rules. He came at Arf, jabbing the broom like a lance. Then he swung it down low, at the knees. Arf had to jump sideways out of the way, up on to the rockery. But Jim came shambling after him, a fiendish look in his eyes and a crazy grin on his lips. 'I'm a swash-buckling pirate!' he shouted. 'You haven't a hope, lad, surrender, or else I shall slice off your head!'

Then Arf got a hasty jab in. Jim Gulliver clutched at his tummy. 'Eeeeh gods, I am wounded,' he bellowed. So Arf pushed home his advantage. His second jab was higher up, though hardly made any contact because Jim tried to lurch back, and in his big leather sandals on those loose lumps of rock he somehow lost his balance. He went tumbling back with his arms flailing out, crashing down into the pond.

The splash soaked all four girls. They jumped about screaming and gasping. Then everyone was gathering round, trying to fish Jim out.

'Oh Arf, *now* what have you done?' cried Mum, hurrying out of the kitchen door, with Janie Gulliver close on her heels, holding her hands to her face.

'He stabbed Mr Gulliver,' Gloria cried. 'Jim's bleeding to death in the pond.'

'I never! It wasn't my fault, Mum.'

'Jim, are you allright?' blathered Janie.

'We should call a doctor,' said Bee.

'An ambulance,' Gloria wailed.

'Yeah, 999's fastest,' said Arf.

'It's not an emergency, Arf,' said Mum, not sounding completely convinced.

Jim dragged himself from the pond, using his hands and one leg. He rolled on to his back on the bank and set about touching his knee.

'Does it hurt at all, dear?' Janie asked him.

Jim seemed to be shaking his head, though also gritting his teeth. He let out his breath in a whistle. 'I'll tell you one thing.'

'What's that, dear?'

He grinned, but only with pain. 'Forget about catching that ferry. This leg will need hospital treatment.'

No one else spoke for a moment.

Then Gloria exclaimed, in a tragic voice that warbled, close to breaking 'Oh Arf – you see what you've managed to do? You've ruined our holiday. *Thanks*!'

Chapter Three

In the end it was Mum who drove Jim along to the hospital, leaving Mrs Gulliver to make sure the girls were okay. Arf had to go with Mum. He sat in the car in silence, thinking how typical, that just when he had an idea to make up for not going camping (and make some money, maybe), something like this had to happen – and everyone tried to blame him!

'Cheer up,' said Jim, 'it serves me right. I forgot where to put my own feet!'

But none of them felt too cheerful after a couple of hours waiting at Casualty. Then a doctor looked at the leg, poked it and waggled Jim's foot, and gave Jim an x-ray. He told them the leg wasn't broken but said something about 'a torn ligament' that Arf didn't understand. The doctor bandaged the leg with splints and lent Jim a pair of crutches. 'Best stay in bed for the first few days, and don't move around too much, at least for the next two weeks.'

'I was meant to be going on holiday, Doc.'

'Not any more,' grinned the doctor, 'you're going to have a good rest.'

* * *

Next morning Arf woke late. So late that everyone else had finished their breakfast before he got out of bed. When he came down for his breakfast, he noticed how peaceful it was.

The girls were out in the garden, with Sam and Susie Gulliver. Mum had asked them over to stay, to give their mum more time for looking after Jim. 'They're making the best of things' she said. 'As they're not going camping in France any more, they're going to camp here, in the garden.'

Arf could hardly believe this. He thought of explaining to Mum that he had got plans for the garden, but that would be just a big waste of breath so he rushed outside instead.

The girls had put up *four* tents. One little one each, down beyond the pond, but taking up half the garden. And now they were all in a huddle, sprawled on a big green ground sheet, giggling – at him, most likely.

'Hi Arf, come and join us,' called Bee.

'No way,' he replied. 'It's illegal, setting up camp without asking.'

'What's illegal about it?' said Bee.

'You didn't want me to come to France, so why should I let you camp here?'

'It's not a question of letting us, Arf. It's *our* garden,' said Gloria sweetly.

'And if it's your campsite,' said Bee, 'you're going to want campers and tents, right? So we're your first campers!'

'I'll charge you!'

They all started squealing so loudly that Mum came rushing out. 'Oh *now* what? Stop it, at once, Arf!'

'I never started anything, Mum. In fact, I was the one who tried to stop it!'

'What were you trying to stop, Arf?'

He tried his best to explain, but the girls butted in, all shouting, so he was forced to shout in order to make himself heard. Until Mum, shouting loudest, tried to make them shut up by saying it would be fair if the girls had half of the garden, and Arf could have the rest, so he could put his own tent up.

'He hasn't got a tent' put in Gloria.

'I was going to make one' said Arf. 'And ask round some friends, maybe, and also customers too.'

'That's fine,' said Mum, 'I don't care what you do, so long as it's up this end, nearest the house. That's your half. But no more quarrels, OK? I've got a great deal to do at the park, helping to set things up. So later on you can come to the park and perhaps even make yourselves useful.'

With that she went back to the kitchen.

Then Gloria said in a lazy tone, 'How long will you have to wait, Arf, before your first "customers" come?'

Both the Gulliver girls giggled.

'A week?' Sammy said.

'Two weeks?' said Sue.

Arf didn't get cross, he stayed cool and calm. 'Less than a day, more likely.'

Gloria spluttered with laughter. 'How much do you want to bet, Arf?'

'Don't fall for it, please,' begged Bee, 'You'll end up with even more debts, Arf.'

'Not if I win,' said Arf, 'And I bet you I do ...'

'No,' gasped Bee.

'All that you owe me' said Gloria, with a cruel smile on her lips. 'That means, if you lose the bet, Arf, you'll owe me twice as much.'

She held out her hand and Arf shook it. She nodded, extra slowly. 'That's four weeks' pocket money.'

* * *

Arf couldn't afford to lose four weeks pocket money. He had to make sure that he won. But how was he going to do that?

At first he simply paced up and down, wondering how many tents could be put on one small bit of lawn? And then he went up to his room and started to write out a list: 'How to set up a campsite.'

You didn't need much, just a flat bit of grass and maybe a water supply. No problem – there was an outside tap that Mum used for watering plants. As for the other facilities, they were dead easy as well, because they were in the house. For instance, there was the bathroom. He only hoped Mum wouldn't mind too much, having loads of strangers trapsing up the stairs to take showers and use the loo. But if she was out in the park every day, arranging this festival week, she wouldn't be here to care ...

As soon as Mum and the girls set off to go to the park he put up some signs with arrows pointing at the back door. Then he went into the house and put a sign saying 'TV Room' on the door to the lounge. Then he went upstairs to put up a couple more signs. He drew a figure on each, to stand for a man and a woman. But they ended up looking the same, so just to make it clearer, so there would be no mess-ups, Arf wrote 'MEN' and 'WOMEN' in thick felt tip, underneath. He stuck both signs on one door, because there was only one bathroom.

Now what? He needed a proper sign to go outside the house to show that this was a campsite and not just an ordinary house. But what should he call the campsite? 'Arf's Big Open Space'? That didn't sound right, somehow.

'Arf's Special Festival Camping'?

That sounded too serious.

What about 'Arf's Fun Camping'?

Or, better still, 'ARF'S HAPPY CAMPING'?

He wrote these words in green paint and drew a happy face. Then he stuck up his sign on the gate outside, adding a few more arrows, just to make totally sure the customers came to the right front door and not to the next door neighbour. Mr Bill Bott was a very good friend to Arf, but he might try to take advantage and ask them into his garden and let them camp there for free.

* * *

Now what?

Arf sat on the doorstep for almost half an hour but not one camper turned up. He got so bored he went back indoors, but there was nothing to do, except go in the 'TV Room', where there was nothing to do, except turn on the telly and eat a packet of crisps. He was on his third packet of crisps when he heard the front door bell chime.

For a moment he thought the girls had come back. He leapt up, switched off the telly and hiding the three empty packets under a cushion, went off to open the door.

A man was on the doorstep. He was short and plump, with long ginger hair and big round spectacles. He grinned at Arf. 'Umm, excuse me, I'm not sure I've got the right place?'

'Right place for who?' said Arf.

'Not who but *what*' said the man, with a wink and a sort of smirk. 'A quiet neck of the green woods, perchance with a grassy clearing, on which to pitch our home for the night and lay our weary heads.'

Whatever was this twit on about?

'In other words, dare I say, campsite?'

Arf stared at him. 'You want to camp here?'

'That's my fondest hope,' said the man. 'We hail from far away, we have had a long day on the road. We're knackered, to put it politely, so you will have saved our lives.' And he gestured at a thin woman standing by the front gate. She was wearing round spectacles too, but also a long, flowery dress. A pale little boy held her hand. An old camper van was behind them.

'Harold's my name,' said the man, holding a chubby hand out. 'Harold Burwash, and yon stands my wife, who goes by the name of Carole, with Ethelred, son and heir. And Matilda, our trusty bus.'

'You can't get that in the garden,' said Arf, his hopes all suddenly dashed. 'It won't go through the side gate!'

'Fear not, we have brought our tents.'

Arf grinned with relief. 'That's all right, then.'

He led them through the house, showing them the TV Room and the stairs leading up to the 'MEN' and 'WOMEN' signs. Then he showed them his patch of green grass.

'Oh dear, is that all?' said Carole.

'How many tents have you got?' said Arf.

'Only the three,' said Harold, 'but somewhat on the sturdy side, not being of modern design. Though each can sleep six happy pilgrims.'

Arf made up his mind, very quickly, he'd charge for the 'pilgrims', not tents. That way, instead of charging for three, he could charge for – hold on – eighteen! And if they stayed the whole week that was eighteen times seven and that was a lot – enough to pay off his debts and buy the table football, and what with winning the bet as well, he might even have enough to take Mum off for a well-earned break – their very own camping trip!

He was hopping about with excitement. 'But where are the other pil– people?'

'We'll just go and fetch 'em,' said Harold.

* * *

As soon as the Burwash family had got itself back in Matilda and gone rattling off down the street, Arf gave a great whoop of glee.

He had got his first eighteen campers. Just wait till Gloria heard! But why should she have to wait? No need to hang about here. The campers could put their own tents up. So, leaving the garden gate open, Arf set off for the park.

Chapter Four

The festival had begun. Most of the stalls were open and people were milling around the park.

There was even an old-fashioned waggon, with 'Gumpy's Famous Steam Organ' emblazoned in colourful letters, letting off a great rip-roaring noise, and a van selling candyfloss. The football pitch at the end was now an enormous car park, leaving only one small open space reserved as a kiddies' play zone.

Only now did Arf remember his bright idea for the dummies. He wondered how well Slash had dressed them up as Ms Vespy and the headteacher? But hold on, something was wrong here. Where was the coconut shy?

The coconut shy had vanished. In its place was a huge marquee that had only just been erected. Some workmen were banging in tent pegs. Arf peered in through the doorway, half expecting to see the coconut shy. Instead he caught sight of Gloria and Bee, along with Sammy and Sue.

'Where's Slash?' he called. 'Where's Ricko?'

Bee pointed out of the doorway, across to the water fountain, where some of the boys from the fencing club were standing around looking glum.

Arf hurried over. 'What happened?'

They told him how they had got to the stall as soon as the park gates opened, only to find Ms Vespy with the mayor from their twin town in France wanting to set up a stall.

'Ms Vespy thought they weren't coming until later on in the week,' Ricko said, 'but Jim Gulliver got the dates wrong, so that left her with the problem of where to put their marquee. It takes up the space of two stalls, and there was only one space that was left – next to our coconut shy...'

'But we had a right to our stall' said Arf.

'We did have' said Slash, 'Till she noticed ...'

'... your bright idea' said Ricko. 'Thanks to that twit of a French boy saying we'd made the dummy look like her. So then she fetched the headteacher. And *he* saw the other dummy that looked like him, of course. He said that was disgraceful, and we didn't deserve our own stall!'

'So it was your fault, Arf,' said Slash.

Arf got a sinking feeling, as he always did when people tried to blame him. 'Hold on a bit' he told Ricko and Slash. 'There's something I've got to find out.'

Inside the marquee he found Bee. 'What's going on? What are you all up to?'

'We're going to help the French,' said Bee. 'Tomorrow they're giving out wine and we'll be waitresses for them!'

'How much will they pay you?' said Arf.

'They don't have to pay us,' said Bee. 'The wine will be free. It's a way to make friends with people from France. They're so nice.'

'So where are they now, your "new friends"?' said Arf.

Bee pointed across at a fat man in shorts

behind a trestle table. 'That's Monsieur Beurre – he's the mayor – and that's his son, Patou.'

Monsieur Beurre had a droopy moustache. Patou was a fat boy in shorts. They were carefully taking glasses out of a cardboard box and lining them up on a tray.

'I've met them before,' Arf muttered, 'down at the supermarket. They were buying their wine!'

'Don't be silly. They've only just got here,' said Bee. 'They came in the night, on the ferry.'

'But I saw them yesterday,' Arf went on. 'Their wine's not even French, it's called Kanga Whatsit. It's on offer.'

'You want to bet on it, Arf?' Gloria said.

'Yes – no.' He remembered something and gave her a nasty grin. 'I've got some good news. My first campers have come, so when are you going to pay me?'

Gloria looked at him coldly. 'Your friends from school don't count, Arf.'

He opened his mouth, then closed it. Much better to let her wait until she had seen for herself! In any case, what was more urgent was getting Monsieur Beurre's son to pay for the bottle he'd broken. But as he called, 'Excuse me, *excusez-moi*, Pat-ooh ...'

The French boy looked up and did it again, he poked his tongue out at Arf, just like at the supermarket. But this time Arf did it back. He stuck his tongue right out, only to see the fat father staring back over Patou's shoulder.

'Oh, Arf, you're so rude,' exclaimed Bee.

'Your wine's not French is it?' Arf asked the man.

Before he knew what was happening, Arf found himself seized by the collar, and booted from the marquee.

* * *

Slash helped Arf back on his feet. 'You all right?'

Arf thought there were no bones broken, or ligaments torn. 'Just unfair,' he gasped. He wanted to find his mum, to get her to lodge a complaint because there had been an assault.

'Why, what did you say,' asked Slash, 'about our coconut shy?'

'I just said his wine wasn't French,' said Arf

'Not funny,' said Slash 'to a Frenchman.'

'I'll tell you what's funny,' said Ricko, trying to cheer him up, 'Ms Vespy, trying to speak French. Hah, hah, you should have heard her, she was completely useless!'

Arf grinned. Then he thought of something that really did cheer him up.

'Hey, Slash, I should soon have the money to buy your table football.'

'How much will you pay me?' asked Slash.

'That depends,' said Arf. 'I'll have to look at it first.'

Arf got himself invited back to Slash's house. They played some table football and it was so amazingly good that Arf made Slash an offer. And then they bargained a bit, and Slash said Arf could take it home, as long as he paid the next day.

The table weighed a ton. By the time he had dragged it home Arf felt completely shattered, but he wanted to get it upstairs, so he could set it up. But when he opened the door he found the four girls in his room, all peering out of the window.

'Hey, what do you think you're up to?'

'Just come and see this, Arf,' gasped Bee. 'Intruders have broken in and taken over our garden!'

'They'll try to break in to the house,' Gloria moaned. 'That's why we're hiding up here. I think we should call the police!'

'No, don't be stupid' said Arf, striding across to the window. 'I told you, I've got my first campers.'

Then Arf looked out of the window. The garden was full of strange people wearing what looked like blankets. They were putting up three big tents, but very peculiar tents, made out of rags and skins. The campers had lit a big fire and a black cauldron hung from a tripod. Smoke billowed up in enormous clouds, drifting over the wall into the neighbouring gardens.

Not quite what he had expected but … no doubt about it! 'I've won the bet. You've got to pay me!'

Gloria grabbed his shoulders and gave him a violent shake: *'You'll* pay for this Arf, when Mum comes home. How could you have done this? They're *freaks*!'

Chapter Five

When Mum came home from the park, Gloria was waiting to tell her the terrible news. 'It's not safe to go in the garden, Mum, because of what Arf has done.'

'Oh, no, what is it this time?' said Mum.

Gloria gave her the goriest details, about a naked child paddling in the pond, and a giant man with a beard sharpening a twin-bladed knife. 'I'm not going to sleep here tonight, Mum, unless the police have removed them!'

'But I sent them to camp here,' said Mum.

'*You* sent them?' said Gloria. 'Why?'

'They were going to camp in the park,' Mum explained, 'but sadly they turned up too late. The French people had taken their space.'

'Thanks to Ms Vespy,' said Arf. 'They took our space as well!'

'They came five days early,' said Mum, 'thanks to Jim Gulliver making another muddle over the dates for their visit, so we couldn't fit in the poor Saxons.'

'Saxons?' said Arf. 'No, they're not called

that. Harold's called Burwash, he told me. I went and wrote it down, Mum, in my camping account book, ready for doing the bill.'

'Bill?' echoed Mum. 'Don't be silly. You're not going to charge them a penny!'

Arf's jaw dropped open. 'Why not?'

'Because they've come here as friends. They're taking part in our festival, Arf. They're not going to charge us for that!'

'It sounds like you've lost your bet,' Gloria said.

'I never – they've come to my campsite and—'

'What's that about losing a bet?' put in Mum.

'Just joking,' said Gloria sweetly.

Arf spluttered in total frustration.

'All right, so let me explain,' said Mum. 'Jim asked them to come to the festival because the church in the town was founded in Saxon times. In fact, it's a thousand years old. The people in our back garden belong to the Saxon Society.'

'What's the Saxon Society, Mum?' asked Bee.

Mum told them about its members dressing up as Saxons 'to try to bring history to life.'

'You mean, they're living like that because they *want* to?' said Gloria, in disbelief.

'Like what, dear?'

'Like ... homeless beggars?'

'It's only their weekend hobby. They go round the country in summer, camping in Saxon style tents, putting on displays of how people lived in those days. So when I remembered Arf's clever idea to make our garden a campsite, I thought he'd like them to camp here! Come on. Let's all go in the garden. You can make friends and learn something.'

* * *

Gloria stayed inside, but Bee came out with Hoppa, and Arf introduced her to Harold. 'And Carole. And this boy called Ethel ...'

'Ethel-red,' beamed Harold. 'A very fine Saxon name. But come forth and sit ye all down.'

They sat down on the grass by the fire.

'Meet Vic, our honest blacksmith. And over there, Brother Edmund, and Sister Agnes is washing her feet. We hope you will do us the honour of sharing our humble meal. We make our own wholesome black bread and dunk it in broth,' Harold said. 'But first...' He picked up a lute, strummed a chord and started to warble this song ...

I tell you of the days, my friends,
When England's pleasant land ♫
Was home to free-born Saxon folk,
Before those evil bands
Of warlike Norman conquerors ♫ ♫
Hailing from over the sea, my friends,
Put us under their cruel yoke.

It sounded a little bit strange to Arf (and the
smoke was making his eyes sting). 'What's this
about cruel egg yolks?'

'The Norman yoke,' said Harold, putting
down his lute, 'by which I mean Norman
bondage of innocent Saxon folk. It started in
1066, when the Normans landed near Hastings,
and it's all been downhill ever since.'

'We Saxons were civilised people,' said Vic, a
big man with a big beard. 'We didn't just live in
these draughty old tents. We had nice comfy
mud huts.'

'And drank lots of mead,' said Harold. 'You don't get that in the shops these days. I make it myself from honey.'

'And I make the bread,' said Carole.

'And I do the weaving,' said Agnes, 'to show how to make Saxon clothes.'

'And I'm a blacksmith,' said Vic. 'So I can bend things in iron, and hammer them out. I mend swords too.'

'Swords?' echoed Arf. This was better. 'Do you think you could make me a sword?'

Vic scratched his beard. 'Tell you what, Arf. I'll show you a Saxon sword.'

Vic went and brought it out. It was nothing like the long needle-thin blade Arf used to parry and thrust with. This one was short and stubby.

'For chopping and jabbing,' grinned Vic.

'Not that the Saxons liked fighting,' Brother Edmund insisted, squatting down by the fire. He was wearing a dirty brown robe tied around the waist with a rope.

'But we had to fight for our lives, Arf. Not that it did us much good.'

'The Normans fought dirty,' said Vic. 'Never gave us a chance.'

'They used longbows.' Harold blinked through his specs. 'They fired arrows up in the air, you see, and the arrows came down on us Saxons before we could get to grips and do any honest fighting. And once our lines were broken, the Normans took advantage. They charged us on their horses and used their vicious lances to spear any helpless survivors. Sheer trickery and skullduggery.'

'Never gave us a chance,' said Vic. 'And afterwards, they grabbed England. They took all our land, forced us Saxons to do all their dirty work for them. So we had to grow all the food, and then the Normans ate it!'

'That's why,' said Brother Edmund, squeezing his hands together, 'you will find the words for animals are all good Saxon words like pig and cow and hen. And the words for the meat are all based on French. Like pork and beef and poultry.'

'And ham,' said Harold, 'from *jambon*.'

'The only good thing the Normans brought were rabbits,' said Brother Edmund. 'There wasn't one rabbit in England before the Normans came.'

'What's good about rabbits?' said Vic.

'I keep two as pets,' said Edmund.

Arf was fascinated. He thought of the 'friends from Normandy', with their giant marquee in the park, where there should have been Saxon tents. 'Now they're cheating again!' he said. 'Betchya.'

'Not rabbits?' said Vic.

'No, Normans!' Arf told them about the Normans' wine not being French. 'It's Australian.'

'He's making that up,' said Bee. 'The Normans are really nice people. It's just that Arf was nasty, so he got booted out.'

'Have you looked at the labels?' said Arf.

'Their bottles don't have any labels because they made the wine themselves at their own vineyard,' said Bee. 'That's why they can give it away!'

Arf's eyes boggled at this.

Harold tutted. 'Perhaps they just bought a few bottles of honest Australian wine as presents for friends back home, to make a pleasant change, no doubt, from their normal Norman plonk?'

'The point is,' said Vic, 'I can see Arf's point. Folks aren't going to pay much attention to us, if the Normans are dishing free wine out, wherever it blooming well comes from.'

'You could hand out free mead,' said Bee.

'I haven't got that much,' said Harold.

Vic scratched his beard. 'What else could we try? Some times we do a mock combat, but you need plenty of blokes for that, and most of the blokes who like fighting have gone away on their hols.'

'I like fighting too,' said Arf, waving his arm

about to show what he did with a sword. But before he could say any more, he heard Mum calling his name.

She came up and squeezed his shoulder. 'I think it might be a good idea if you went round to see Jim.'

'I said I was sorry last night, Mum. He even said it was his fault, forgetting where his feet were. '

'I know it wasn't your fault, Arf. I just think you might cheer him up.'

Chapter Six

Jim Gulliver lived only two streets away, but Arf took his time on this walk. He was thinking about mock combat. It would bring together his new Saxon friends and his friends at the fencing club, so they could all have a good fight. Slash would be pleased about that, Arf thought – it would make up for the coconut shy. Mock combat should draw a big crowd too, so they could sell lots of tickets. Arf thought he should take a rake off for being the organiser, but nobody else would allow it, he knew. Why was it so hard to earn money?

Mrs Gulliver opened the door. She looked extremely tired, though Arf could hear Jim in the background, and he was laughing away!

Jim was with Larry, his brother, who was older than him, his sweep of fair hair turning grey. Larry was wearing a paisley cravatte tucked into a bright blue shirt. He beamed up at Arf from an armchair. 'All hail, our swash-buckling hero, I've heard how you did for old Jim, and serves him right too, what a joker!

Forgot where to put his own feet! He'll forget where he's put his own head next. He's a one-man disaster area!'

'Old Jim' was on the sofa, his leg bound up like a mummy, his foot propped up on a stool. He was wearing an old dressing gown. 'Hello, Arf. Want some chocolate?' He broke off six chunks for Arf and shoved another three chunks into his own big mouth. 'It's Belgian luxury chocolate.' He chomped and chomped. 'Larry brought it. I say, do you want some more, Janie?'

'I think we've all had enough, Jim.'

'We've only had half the bar.'

'No, this is the second bar, Jim. You've got a mind like a sieve.'

'Oh, oh,' groaned Jim. 'Any moment she's going to tell us all over again about her birthday treat!'

Larry chuckled and turned back to Arf. 'Janie said she'd always wanted to eat at a local restaurant called the Greedy Gourmet. So Jim went and booked a table at the Gourmand Normand, by mistake.'

'And for the wrong date,' added Janie.

'The food not as good?' wondered Arf.

For some mysterious reason all three of them burst into laughter. Larry ended up using his paisley cravatte to wipe a tear from his cheek. Then Jim said, 'Let's change the subject. How's life at the park?'

Arf told him about the coconut shy, and the Saxons camped in the garden, though he was in such a hurry to talk about the mock combat he might have missed a few details.

'Mock combat! Amazing idea,' groaned Jim. 'It's always been an ambition of mine to take part in an historic battle. Two sides slog it out, a real clash of a fight, like Cavaliers against Roundheads.'

'Or cowboys and indians,' said Janie, in rather

a sarky tone, but Arf didn't notice this.

'It ought to be Saxons v Normans,' said Jim.

'But first find your Normans,' said Larry.

'We've got some already,' said Arf, recalling the wine marquee. 'From our twin town, but they're not up to much. Besides, they're all cheats. They don't fight clean.'

'Hold on,' said Jim, 'You're talking about our new French friends but *they're* not coming until the Saxons have gone, Arf.'

'No, they came today,' Arf corrected him. 'That's why the Saxons can't camp in the park. The thing is, you got the dates wrong.'

'I don't believe this!' cried Janie, clapping her hands to her face.

'Well, neither do I,' said Jim, shaking his head in amazement. 'I tried very hard to arrange things right. I talked to the mayor on the phone.'

'Perhaps you slipped up talking French?' said Arf.

'How could I have done? We spoke English.'

'So maybe his English slipped up then?'

Jim thought about this long and hard. He tried to shift his left leg, as if to get up and do something, only to wince with the pain.

'Well, they're giving away free wine,' said Arf, 'so nobody else seems to mind.'

'Free wine?' said Larry. 'That sounds very nice.'

Arf didn't bother to tell him about the supermarket. Bee might have been right after all. 'Someone said they've got their own vineyard.'

'In Normandy, Arf? I don't think so. They go in for orchards and cider ...'

'I'd better phone up to say I'm sorry,' said Jim. 'And maybe I'll ask him over for later on this evening so we can have a chat. But where's he staying, I wonder. Don't tell me he's camped in your garden?'

'He'll be with Ms Vespy,' said Arf.

'That's it. Yes, I'll give her a call.'

He reached for the phone and dialled a number.

He talked, he listened, he talked. 'No, actually, I'm not phoning from France.' His cheeks went pink. 'Still at home. Twisted my leg as it happens but ... I gather there's been a slight mix-up.' Now even his ears were crimson. And Arf could hear Ms Vespy's voice whining down the line. 'It's been so much work,' she protested. 'We had to find space for their huge marquee, and now I'm putting them up for the night and I'm having to cook the mayor's supper. The French like their food, so it's got to be good, I had to spend a fortune on the Gourmet Frozen Food range down at the supermarket. I'm heating it up in the microwave.' Ping! 'We're just about to sit down and eat, so no, you can't talk to him now! The Mayor might phone you back later.'

'She's put down the phone,' Jim protested.

'Well, that ought to teach you,' said Larry, turning back to Arf. 'Incidentally, I think I can help with your battle. If you come round in the morning, I'll lend you some swords and helmets. You just need someone to bring you, it takes half an hour in the car!'

'Larry runs a theatrical costume store,' Janie Gulliver said to Arf.

'In fact I could take you myself,' said Jim.

'I don't think you could,' said Larry.

'Why not?' Jim thought for a moment, then tapped his bad leg. 'No. Forgot!'

* * *

Arf walked home full of excitement, thinking of swords and shields. Who could give him a lift along to the costume store? Mum would be too busy.

He was at the far end of their street when he saw the front door open. His sisters came out on the step, and then that nasty fat French boy came poncing out of their house, waving and calling *'Bon nuit!'*.

Arf waited until he had gone (the other way down the street) before he approached the front gate. Only then did he notice his sign. Someone had tampered with it!

'Arf's UN-Happy Camping' he read. His smily face had been mucked up too. The smile had been buried under a thick black angry frown.

Arf tore it down in disgust. He chucked it into the gutter. He hated that horrible French boy.

But hold on. As he looked up he noticed the camping bus parked beside the kerb. Matilda seemed to be smiling at him. He remembered the costume store. Why shouldn't Harold take him?

Chapter Seven

Saturday morning dawned bright and clear, with the sun shining in through the window, waking up Arf. Typical! He lay there and thought about how unfair it all was, that he should be running a campsite and yet be the only person (other than Mum, of course) not having spent the night in a tent!

He had left the window wide open to let in the cool night air, and what had got in? Mosquitoes! He was itching all over. He wondered if there had been mosquitoes back in Saxon times, or had the Normans imported them, along with all their rabbits?

And what had they eaten for breakfast? Not Frosties or Cocopops? He reckoned it might be better not to take any risks but have a nice breakfast indoors.

He found Mum down in the kitchen drinking a cup of tea. He told her about his camp sign. She told him to not make a fuss. 'You shouldn't have poked your tongue out at Patou's father, Arf!'

'Patou poked his tongue out at me, Mum, and what was he doing round here?'

'He came to see the girls, Arf. Ms Vespy booted him out. She wanted to give the Mayor a slap-up candle-lit dinner!'

Arf told her how Jim had tried to phone, only to get the brush-off. He poured himself Cocopops and spooned on lots of sugar before Mum could try to stop him, then told her about the mock combat and going to get proper gear from Larry's costume store. 'If Harold's up for it, Mum.'

'I'm sure he will be,' said Mum. 'I've pencilled it into the programme as starting at half-past two, so that leaves you plenty of time.'

* * *

As soon as Mum left the house Arf went out in the garden. He found Harold doing his best to get the fire burning again, pumping away at the embers with a big pair of Saxon bellows.

Ethelred was out on the grass, playing with Saxon bricks (these were made of bare wood, not plastic). Sister Agnes was kneading bread dough to make Saxon rolls for their breakfast. She said she wanted to bake more bread at the festival too.

'If there's room for a campfire,' said Harold, raising a Saxon pot to his lips and taking a thirsty swig.

'Did Saxons have tea and coffee?' asked Arf.

Harold said these had not been discovered.

Then Vic brought out an object that looked a bit like the bagpipes (except that there weren't any pipes). Unscrewing its top he squeezed its sides, filling two more pots with a cloudy, brown frothy liquid. He handed a pot to Arf. 'It's Saxon ale. Very healthy.'

Arf took a small sip and spat it out. It was sour. But the two men seemed to love it. They knocked back several pots. And when Harold got out his lute to strum a Saxon song, Vic joined in to sing the chorus.

In fact, there were plenty more Saxon songs before the Saxon rolls were properly cooked inside (and blackened and charred outside).

Meanwhile the girls got on with enjoying their own special private breakfast. They had croissants and jam, fruit yoghurts and mugs of creamy hot chocolate. Arf looked on in jealous amazement.

'You can't eat all that, it's not Saxon!'

'We're not being Saxons,' said Bee.

'What are you then, Normans?' said Arf.

Gloria glared at him. 'Actually, Arf, it's what we'd have had for breakfast in France, if *you* hadn't spoilt things for us.'

* * *

By the time the Saxons had finished their rolls and loaded the spinning wheel into the back of the bus, it was getting on for mid-morning. The girls had left Hoppa behind. 'You come with me,' said Arf, and Hoppa jumped into the bus.

At the park they found lots of people milling round the marquee. The Normans were open for business. A banner hung over the entrance flap announcing–

YOUR NEW FRIENDS FROM NORMANDY!
Come in and taste our FREE wine!!

Arf peered in through the doorway, expecting to see the fat French boy with his nasty fat father. Instead he caught sight of Gloria, pouring wine into glasses, and Bee cutting up some cheese into small, gooey slices.

As he stepped inside Ms Vespy tapped his shoulder. She was wearing a black and yellow stripy top and she looked like an angry wasp.

'Arf, can't you read?' she demanded.

'About the free wine?' Arf grinned. 'Is that why you've come in here, Miss?'

'Certainly not, I'm too busy. I just came to put up this notice!'

The notice was stuck on a tent pole.

> 'Wine for
> adults only.
> No children
> under 14
> allowed
> inside the
> marquee.'

Typical.

'Actually, Miss,' said Arf, 'I wanted to ask if the Saxons can have some space for their spinning wheel, and light a campfire and so forth, so they can bake Saxon bread?'

'Certainly not,' said Ms Vespy. 'Too much of a safety risk! Jim Gulliver shouldn't have asked them along. And as for this idea of having some sort of "mock combat"—'

Before she could ban that as well, Monsieur Beurre came waddling over with two glasses of wine. He held one out. 'This is for you, *ma cherie. Tu es belle*, and such a good cook.'

She flushed.

'*Ah, comment une rose. Tu es une rose Anglaise!*'

Arf stared at Ms Vespy in wonder. She was suddenly googly and giggling just like a schoolgirl. In fact, it was so disgusting that Hoppa went bounding off with a growl, making a bee-line for Bee, and Arf thought it safest to follow.

'You should have seen that!' he chuckled, helping himself to a chunk of cheese and tossing one down for Hoppa.

'Hoppa shouldn't be in here,' Bee whispered.

'Arf shouldn't be either,' said Gloria. 'Get out of here. This is for grown-ups.'

'I'll go if you pay what you owe for that bet. I need the money for something.'

'You haven't got campers, just Saxons!'

'What's wrong with them being Saxons?'

'They're not paying, neither am I!'

'At least the Saxons are honest,' cried Arf. 'Not like you Norman cheats, mucking up my camping sign and sticking your tongues out at people!'

'Oh, don't be such a baby, Arf. Go and play with your stupid Saxons! "Mock fighting", that's all you're good for!'

'Better than smooching up with that twit!' Arf pointed a finger at Patou. 'He still owes me for that broken bottle!'

Patou had his back to Arf. He was loading a tray with glasses.

'Excuse me. *Excusez-moi*?' said Arf. But Patou completely ignored him.

So Arf went and tapped his shoulder, just as the French boy was lifting the tray. 'That *bouteille de* Kanga-Whatsit' said Arf. 'You've got to *payez-moi*.'

'He speaks better English than you!' Gloria called.

'Let's hear him then,' Arf retorted.

The boy turned, swinging the tray round so the corner jabbed Arf in the chest. It was a painful knock, though he did it so craftily that the glasses of wine hardly trembled. But as he moved back with a nasty grin, he didn't see Hoppa behind him. He trod on Hoppa's front paw.

Hoppa barked and the fat boy jerked, making the glasses wobble. Some of the wine sloshed out.

Arf reached out to steady the tray. But Patou pulled it backwards, making the glasses totter.

They might have been fine, if he'd just let them be, but Patou tried too hard. His fat little eyes blinked wildly, he tried to straighten the tilt, first one way then the other. The tray rocked from side to side. The glasses bumped into each other and then the first glass tripped over. The rest of them might have been saved, but Patou went after the first one, shifting the whole tray to catch it.

There was an incredible smash.

'Oh, Arf,' gasped Bee. '*Now* look what you've done.'

'Get him out of here!' Gloria cried.

'That wasn't my fault,' Arf shouted. 'He just

didn't like me asking about his Australian wine!'

'Arf, whose is that dog' called Ms Vespy.

And for the second time in two days, Monsieur Beurre grabbed Arf by the collar and booted him from the marquee.

And Patou
booted out Hoppa.

So much for the 'friends from Normandy'!

Arf shoved his way through the crowd, with Hoppa close on his heels, wondering where Mum might be. (This time he would lodge a complaint!) But he looked at his watch. Time was pressing. He needed to get a move on.

He found Slash and some of the others across by the potted plant stall run by Mr Bill Bott. They all looked as peeved as he felt. But then Arf told them his news, about the mock combat at 2.30. They took the news very well. Mock combat suited them fine. In fact, they were keen to start practising now, with bamboo canes pulled from pots supporting Mr Bott's plants.

Arf had to stop them. 'Don't do it, because if Ms Vespy sees you she'll say it's a safety risk and she'll try to cancel the combat. I'm going off now for some swords and shields. You set up the ticket office. We're going to make lots of money.'

'Yeah, talking of money,' said Slash, 'about my table football ...'

'I'll sort it out later. Don't worry.'

* * *

Arf climbed in to the camper van and Hoppa jumped in behind him.

Matilda was practically Saxon. She was rusty and stank of petrol. Her engine made frightening noises but couldn't get up enough power to go much faster than a walking pace.

'All in good time,' said Harold, 'The old girl doesn't like rushing, but she'll get us there. Wherever. Do you know where we're meant to be going?'

63

Arf had brought Jim's street map. Larry had marked his costume store with a big 'X' in felt tipped pen. Now Harold studied this map, first one way up then the other, blinking through his round specs. 'Left turn at the end of the road, then straight for most of the way – it should take about twenty minutes. As long as we don't get tangled up by too many one-way streets. They always seem to wreak havoc with even the best-laid plans.'

And he was right about this. The journey took over an hour. Matilda was burbling and bubbling.

'I think she's on fire,' said Arf.

'Just letting off steam,' said Harold. 'The old girl doesn't like traffic, it makes her get hot around the collar. By the time we have picked up our swords and our shields she'll be right as rain. Don't you worry.'

* * *

Larry's costume store took up the top floor of an old warehouse building. At first Arf thought there was nobody there, but when he called out, Larry answered from the very far corner, behind a sewing machine. He was stitching some sort of costume.

'Got ripped on stage,' Larry said, 'in *The Revengers Tragedy*. It could have been worse but, lucky for me, the poppers popped. Goodness me!' He broke off, staring at Harold who was wearing his Saxon jerkin. 'That looks a bit on the home-made side.'

'All Saxon clothes were home-made,' Harold said. 'No gizmos like zips or poppers.'

'But zippers and poppers are blessings, dear boy. Can't think how you'd manage without them,' Larry said.

Harold stared at him through his round specs.

'So what about swords and shields?' said Arf.

'How many d'you need?' asked Larry. 'I also do a good line in very fine chain mail vests.'

'Saxons never wore chain mail vests,' Harold said, 'It was a Norman gimmick.'

'So the Normans should wear them' said Arf. 'To make it look like a real battle!'

But Harold did not look happy. 'You can't expect honest Saxons to dress up like Normans, Arf. They won't do it. Point of honour.'

'In that case,' Arf decided, 'I'll have to get the fencing club to play the part of the Normans.'

'We can't have them winning the fight, Arf.'

'That's true.' Arf scratched his head. 'So I'll be a Saxon with Slash, because he's the fencing champion. That way, we'll win. It's dead simple.'

'The Battle of Hastings Take Two!' Larry beamed. 'If only my brother could be there. He'd make a good, honest Saxon!'

'He doesn't like Normans?' asked Harold.

'Just one particular Norman – the chef at the Gourmand Normand.

'Why? What did he do?' asked Harold.

'That's a long story.' said Larry. 'But come along, back to business.'

Larry was eager to show them all his amazing clobber. There were racks of military uniforms – scarlet jackets with bright brass buttons and hefty loops of gold braid. There were belts and boots and muskets and piles of dusty grey wigs, and loads of ladies' dresses with bustles and low-cut busts. Finally Larry guided them into a room full of armour, with breastplates and helmets with visors, and spears and lances and axes. And stacks of shields in various shapes, and bundles of all sorts of swords.

It was like a fun supermarket. Arf loaded up a trolley, and Larry wrote down what he took.

> 20 short Saxon swords.
> 15 long Norman swords.
> 20 round Saxon shields.
> 15 long Norman shields.
> 20 Saxon helmets.
> 15 Norman helmets with
>   nose guards.

Harold picked up a chain mail vest. 'It's heavy. I wouldn't wear one, not if you paid me Arf! It would slow a man down in battle.'

Arf grinned. 'Good reason to take some and make the Normans wear them!'

They were loading the vests in to Matilda when Larry's mobile phone bleeped. 'Hello, hello? Arf, it's Jim. He wants you to drop in and see him. He's got something 'shocking' to tell you – about that Norman mayor!'

Chapter Eight

As they drove back down the street, Matilda was shaking and shuddering so much that Arf couldn't read the map, let alone try to work out what Jim's shocking news might have been.

Harold turned on the windscreen wipers. The washer produced no water. 'Can't see where I'm going,' he grumbled.

'That's because of the smoke,' said Arf.

'It's not smoke. It's steam,' said Harold.

But then Matilda gave a wild lurch, and her engine coughed and died, and Harold had to turn the wheel to draw her up by the kerb.

'You can't stop here,' said Arf. 'It's a double yellow line.'

'No choice,' Harold said. 'Old girl's thirsty. We'll need to find her some water.'

Looking across the street, Arf noticed a restaurant. It was ten past one already, so he guessed it ought to be open.

He left Harold fanning his hands up and down, trying to clear the steam and have a look under the bonnet.

The restaurant door was wide open. Arf came face to face with a waiter. The waiter did not look too pleased, especially when he saw Hoppa. He asked if Arf wanted a table.

'No. Could I just have some water?'

'We do not sell drinks by themselves, sir. Only with food.'

This was tricky. Arf was wondering if Harold would stretch to a snack? But then he caught sight of the menu. It wasn't the sort of menu for burgers or slices of pizza. It was like a large photo album. It had a thick leather cover. On the cover, in loopy gold letters, was the name of the place. Arf took a deep breath, for this was the Gourmand Normand!

But before he could scoot and tell Harold, the chef barged out of the kitchen, holding a rolling pin. 'A customer! Please take a seat!'

'You're English?' gulped Arf.

'Australian.'

'But I thought–' He glanced at that menu again to make sure he'd read it correctly.

'We've only been here a few days,' said the chef, 'we just haven't changed the name yet. Though goodness knows, we'll sure have to!'

'Because it sounds Norman?' said Arf.

The Australian laughed. 'Not that simple. We got this place on the cheap, but we only got the full story about why we got it so cheap when we talked to some local people. And one of them showed me this.' He moved back behind the bar and brought out a newspaper cutting. 'It's out of the local paper.'

Arf saw a smudgy photograph of a man with a sweep of fair hair holding an envelope.

'I know him,' gasped Arf. 'It's Jim Gulliver!'

Then he read the article.

Reader's letter brings a rotten reaction

Local man, Jim Gulliver, got more than he bargained for at a posh French restaurant, the Gourmand Normand, in Low Street. He was taking his wife, Janie, for a special celebration to mark her fortieth birthday, but it all went disastrously wrong.

'We plumped for the seafood starter,' said Jim. 'But the prawns and the mussels were bad. You could tell by the awful smell. We only ate three or four.

'And then our steaks were charred to a flake. My bit was actually smouldering. I had to complain again. Then the chef came out in a towering rage and said it was all my fault, wanting to have it "well done".

"This isn't well done, it's been blow-torched" I said.

'Well, after another half hour the waiter brought out two more steaks. But when we cut into them we found they were raw inside. Our plates were swimming with blood. So we had to complain again. Then the chef went really crazy, calling us English pigs and ignorant scum with no taste for good food, not worth getting out of his bed for.

'I had to stand up for myself. I said, "That's all very well, but I go to France every summer, I know about real French food. I'm even organising for the mayor from our twin town in Normandy, to come to our town festival! Though actually, I won't be there at the time, I'll be on my holiday then. But that doesn't make any difference. My point is, no need to be rude!"

'This didn't go down

very well with Chef. In fact, that's an understatement. He actually shook his cleaver less than an inch from my nose. 'Get out' he screamed, 'Or I'll show you how rude a real Frenchman can be!'

'So off we went, I can tell you and wrote to the paper about it. But blow me down, two days later, after my letter was published, and after we were still getting over the food poisoning caused by those mussels, I woke up to find sacks of rubbish emptied all over the doorstep.

'There were stinking prawns and mussels still sticking to frozen food packs. And bits of charred steak, and the raw steak too, crawling with maggots and blow flies! I called in the food hygiene people. They had a poke through the packaging. Turned out it was all past its sell-by date by weeks, if not months, so they got him. They're bringing a case against him. I just hope it makes him close down!'

'Oh wow!' said Arf.

'That's what I thought. We've not had one customer yet. I think we'll spend this evening trying to dream up a new name. Hold on though, is that your dad?' He pointed across the street.

Harold was by Matilda, (still steaming away like a smoke bomb), but now he was also having to deal with a female traffic warden. Her pen hovered over her notepad.

'Unusual clothes,' said the waiter.

'He's not my dad. He's a Saxon,' said Arf. 'We're meant to be taking part in a festival held in our park. At this rate we'll miss our own battle.'

'Not fighting the Normans?'

'You bet.'

'In that case,' said the waiter, rubbing his hands together, 'we'd both be delighted to help!'

'Let's get you a barrel of water' said Chef, 'And then you can be on your way!'

* * *

'Thank goodness for that' said Harold, as they pulled back in to the traffic. The old girl's a bit overheated but should get us home in one piece.'

The trouble was they got lost, but after another half hour or so they finally passed the turning that led to Arf's house.

'Hold on, I've still got to go and see Jim!'

'I can't risk waiting' said Harold, aware of the first wisps of steam curling up out of the bonnet. 'I'll drop you off and I'll go on. Then people can have their swords and their shields, and everyone will be ready to fight just as soon as you get there.'

* * *

Arf knocked on Jim's front door.

Janie Gulliver let him in. She looked even paler than usual. 'We're all in a right state here' she said, 'but come in, Jim wants to tell you something.'

Jim was cradling the telephone, his leg propped up on the stool. 'Outrageous,' he cried when he caught sight of Arf. 'Oh Arf, you're not going to believe this.'

Arf wanted to tell him his news, about the Gourmand Normand, but Jim never left him a moment.

'Quite gobsmacked, I don't get it! I've just phoned Ms Vespy to warn her, but she thinks I'm out of my head. If only. But somebody else is.'

'Calm down and explain,' soothed his wife.

The story came out. 'Last night' said Jim, 'Monsieur Beurre didn't call me back. So first thing this morning I tried again. Just wanted to say I was sorry. But would Ms Vespy let me? Came out with all this nonsense about him being too angry, too disappointed in me. That got me down, I can tell you, coming from her, of all people. But then I thought, Hold on, Jim, I've got the Mayor's mobile number! He said it would work here in England. Let's try that, he'll have to answer, then I'll give him my side of the story! It rings a few times, the Mayor answers.'

"Bonjour, Jim," he says. "Bonnes vacances? How do you like camping in France?" That throws me. Makes me wonder if Ms Vespy passed on my message?

'I tell him I've injured my leg, or else I'd be

74

down in the park so he could give me my free glass of wine! But he doesn't get the joke. He says he's not down in a park.

'In that case, where are you?' I ask him.

'In my house in St Aubert,' he tells me.

Arf shook his head. Was Jim joking? 'He can't have got home to France, Jim. He was in the park first thing this morning.'

'No, that's where you're wrong,' said Jim. 'The Monsieur Beurre I talked to on his mobile phone said he hasn't set off. He's coming on Thursday, as planned.'

'So which Monsieur Beurre has come here then?'

'That's a very good question,' said Jim.

Chapter Nine

Arf ran at top speed to the park, with Hoppa bounding behind him. All the way, he was asking himself if Jim's leg injury had gone to his head and given him funny dreams?

How could there be two Monsieur Beurres, and where did this second one come from, if not from the Norman twin-town? Why else was he wasting his time here, giving away free wine?

Then Arf caught sight of his mum, outside the park gate, selling tickets. He wanted to tell her about it. But she didn't want to listen.

'Please Arf. This is all very silly. You're just trying to make up a story because Monsieur Beurre kicked you out of his tent for being a horrible nuisance!'

'I'm not! It's not me at all, mum. It's *him* and this is what Jim said—'

'Just leave him alone to get better, and go off and play with your swords.'

Hah! What sort of put-down was that? But Arf had no time to delay. It was twenty past two already. Though at the kiddies' play zone all he could see were three Saxons (wearing Saxon helmets), and a couple of sulky mums with kids booted out of the play zone.

Harold, Vic and Slash were there, but where was Brother Edmund? Where were the other fencers who ought to be wearing chain mail vests?

'They're all in *that* tent,' said Harold, pointing towards the marquee which seemed to be full to bursting, with people pushing and shoving, all shouting and laughing and ... drinking.

'The wine's been flowing all morning,' said Vic.

'How many tickets d'you sell, Slash?'

'None yet,' said Slash. 'If they get free wine people aren't going to pay for a battle. They think we should give that away too.'

'We can't have much of a battle, with only four fighters,' said Arf.

'We could have a duel' said Vic. 'Two blokes slog it out. Best man wins.'

'Then have a quick whip round?' said Arf.

'I'm game,' said Slash. 'Take you on, Arf? You want to be Saxon or Norman?'

'I'm Saxon' said Arf, quickly reaching out for a Saxon helmet and shield.

'No, you've got to be Norman,' said Harold. 'We can't have a Saxon defeated, not as our opening number.'

Arf didn't like this one bit. 'Can't you find

someone else to be Norman?'

Vic said that none of the Saxons wanted to dress up as Normans. 'The only people who liked the idea were that pair from the French marquee. But just to dress up – they won't fight us, because they're our *notres amis*.'

Just then a great cheering broke out from inside the Norman marquee, and Brother Edmund rushed out, face flushed from sampling the wine. 'It's free wine for life!' he shouted. 'And all for a few hundred pounds!'

'What on earth does that mean?' Harold grumbled. 'He's squiffy; he's losing his marbles.'

But Arf had to find out more. This Monsieur Beurre was a mystery. And he intended to solve it. He poked his head in through the flaps.

* * *

Inside the marquee it was hot and lots of people were drinking lots of glasses of wine, but something else was happening. There was a queue. 'Monsieur Beurre' was wearing a helmet with a long Norman noseguard that prodded his droopy moustache, as well as a vest of chain mail. He was standing under a banner that said Chateau Rou de la Crique.

His fat son was wearing a helmet too. He was handing out forms to people and people were filling them in. Then people were getting out money – very thick wads of money.

Arf sidled across to Bee. 'What's going on now?' he demanded.

But she didn't have to tell him because 'Monsieur Beurre' spoke out, 'Roll up, roll up, your very last chance. Invest in a share of our vineyard. In return for a modest investment you will receive free wine for the whole of the rest of your life! Best deal of the century. Prestige wine. Special offer as friends of twin-town. Sixty fine bottles of wine every year. You cannot regret it. Roll up!'

'Fetch Mum,' cried Gloria. 'Quickly!'

But Bee was tugging his arm. 'Hey, Arf, is Hoppa all right? Where is he? He isn't with you?'

Hoppa had disappeared.

'I hope that horrible Patou didn't hurt Hoppa,' said Bee. 'Since Hoppa got kicked I've been thinking about what you said they'd been up to.'

'Oh yeah?' said Arf, juggling figures. Sixty fine bottles. How much would they cost, down at the supermarket?

'About the Australian wine, Arf!'

Arf was still doing his sums.

'I searched through the waste bin, Arf, and –'

Hundreds of pounds, thought Arf. Then Sue and Sammy were calling to Bee that their Uncle Larry was here. 'He's brought Dad along, in his car!'

Arf heard this. He needed to tell them about Monsieur Beurre's crazy offer. It sounded too good to be true – something had to be dodgy about it.

He pushed his way back through the crowd, out of the open marquee. Larry's sports car was blocking the way between the marquee and the play zone.

Ms Vespy was standing in front of it like a traffic warden. 'It's not allowed. You must move it. This car is a safety risk.'

'But I've got permission,' said Larry. 'The nice lady by the park gate gave me an invalid pass.'

'But you're not an invalid!'

'Certainly not.' Larry gestured towards the car. 'My brother is. Look at his leg.'

The passenger seat had been pushed right back to make enough space for the leg. It stuck straight out on to the dashboard, thick and white like a snowman's leg.

'Hello, Arf!' called Jim. 'I got Larry to bring me along. Couldn't wait. I had to get to the bottom of this mystery about the suspicious Frenchman. I wonder, could you ask him over?'

Arf looked in through the flap. 'Monsieur Beurre' was standing up now, on the trestle table, the top of his Norman helmet brushing against the banner, and even from here they could hear, loud and clear—

'The last three shares, my good English friends, in our great, famous vineyard, will go to the highest bidder. May I open the bidding, yes, over there—'

Arf suddenly had a strange thought. He turned quickly back to Ms Vespy. She was the French teacher at school, after all. 'Excuse me, Miss,' he demanded, 'But you should know.

What's a *'rou'*?'

Her pointy nose twitched. She looked puzzled.

'I mean, like up on that banner. In French, it says, Chateau la "rou".'

'Oh. Surely you must remember that, Arf! We did that in class. It means "road".'

'I thought that's spelt "rue"?'

Her cheeks flushed. 'Yes, "roue" means "wheel" then.'

'That's, "roue" with an "e" Larry said.

'So?' Arf persisted.

Ms Vespy glared.

'What about the last word on the banner?'

'Oh shut up, Arf, please,' snapped Ms Vespy.

'*Une crique*?' Larry said. 'That's dead easy. The same as in English, dear boy.'

'Creek, that explains it,' gasped Arf. 'Chateau "le Rou" like in "kanga-rou".'

'Kangaroo ends with "o"' snarled Ms Vespy.

'Not in French, it doesn't,' said Larry.

Arf dived back in the marquee. He pushed towards Monsieur Beurre and his son. Patou flicked his tongue out.

'Don't give them your money,' he blurted. 'The whole thing's a con. You'll be cheated!'

'Arf, stop it!' Gloria shouted.

But Arf couldn't stop it. Not now.

'These twits haven't got any vineyard,' he

yelled. 'They're not even from St Aubert!'

'So where do you think they are from?' demanded the headteacher. 'You can't say things like that Arf, unless you can prove it. So can you?'

The noise level dropped to zero. All eyes were on Arf. All at once he wasn't so sure of himself. Supposing he'd got this wrong?

Then a sort of fluttering murmur built up round the marquee as people started to whisper.

'It's very good wine … such a bargain … free wine for the rest of our lives … I really don't see what the catch could be … Where else would they get their wine from …'

'Well, go on,' called Bee. 'Tell them, Arf! It's three for the price of two, you said, down at the supermarket.'

He nodded. Whose side was she on?

Monsieur Beurre jabbed a finger at Arf. 'This boy is just out to make trouble. He puts out his tongue, he breaks glasses, and now he comes telling these lies.'

'He's not telling lies.' Bee shouted. 'I found the proof, show him, Arf?'

'What's that?' said Arf.

'In the waste bin.'

Arf half remembered something that Bee had been trying to tell him. Of course! What else could it be but a bottle of Kanga Creek, with the label still on? That would prove it!

He rushed across, grabbed the bin and hurried back, turning it upside down to empty it on to the table in front of Monsieur Beurre.

But not one bottle rolled out.

There was nothing but bits of paper. Arf stared at the mess in dismay.

He guessed the mayor had been too quick – he'd had time to hide the bottles.

'So what does that prove?' said Ms Vespy. 'It proves you are a naughty boy.'

'Who makes lots of trouble,' said Monsieur Beurre 'for your nice Norman friends.

And Patou put his tongue out.

Arf wanted to just disappear. He looked down as the headeacher said, 'We'll have a word later, young man.'

But then Arf saw two words on one of those pieces of paper. He looked again, just to make sure. And a third time, to be certain. Then he waved the piece of paper in front of the headteacher.

'Hold on – look at this – it's the label.'

'They steamed them all off,' cried Bee.

The headteacher blinked in amazement and read out loud 'Kanga Creek'.

* * *

After that everything happened very fast.

'Monsieur Beurre' grabbed hold of the cash box. He vaulted right over the table. Arf blocked his path and he had his short Saxon sword, but 'Monsieur Beurre' kept going. Arf got in one swing with his sword, then the fat man piled into Arf like a bull charging through a farm gate. He wore his chain mail vest which made him extremely heavy. He knocked Arf right out of the way.

But the blow from Arf's sword must have caught 'Monsieur Beurre' a hefty whack on the wrist. The cash box flew out of his hand, and as it went up in the air, the lid opened, spilling out banknotes. Then everyone was closing in, fighting to get back their money.

'Monsieur Beurre' waded on through the crowd. Pushing, heaving and shoving, knocking aside stray Saxons, he burst out from the marquee and blundered past Larry's sports car. He went charging into the play zone.

He would have got away, except that the zone had been cordoned off with a stout orange rope secured to stout wooden posts. He came bouncing back with a yell, went tumbling down on his bottom, and the Saxons all piled on top.

Then Arf was after Patou.

The fat boy could certainly run. What stopped

him came out of the crowd, shooting past Arf with a yowl and overtaking Patou.

Hoppa! The little dog spun round on two paws showing his teeth and growling.

Patou grabbed a sword from the ground – one of Larry's long Norman swords. He swung it about and he prodded, doing his best to spear Hoppa. The little dog jumped out of range, but wouldn't give up. He kept circling, closing in then dodging back as the French boy tried to get him.

Arf just had his short Saxon sword. The rule of the fencing club was 'Never fight with an untrained swordsman except in self-defence'. But this was in Hoppa's defence, so Arf had to fight him and win!

Patou lashed out with his sword, swinging it left and right, but Arf could parry and thrust. Sword struck sword – once, twice, then the Norman sword snapped in half. It was made of painted plywood.

Patou threw it down in disgust. But before he could turn and run, Hoppa closed in again, and with an enormous bound caught the boy by the back of his shorts, holding on tight with his teeth.

Patou tried to wriggle, he struggled, he tried to break free, but his shorts just slipped further down.

'Don't let that dog bite me' he shouted.
He put his hands up 'I surrender'.

* * *

The fake 'Monsieur Beurre', was still on the ground, winded and belly side up, with Harold and Vic, Brother Edmund and Slash, all sitting on him in a line as if they were on a park bench. He was dripping with sweat. He was panting for breath, eyes boggling at Larry's red sports car.

His head lolled back and the helmet flicked off, along with the curly black hair. It was a wig. He was bald underneath. And Jim called to Arf, 'Good heavens, I've suddenlty twigged! It's the chef from the Gourmand Normand who dumped all that mess on my doorstep!'

Chapter Ten

It didn't take long after that to work out what was behind this.

The chef had a grudge against Jim for wrecking his restaurant business.

'I am a fool,' Jim admitted. 'I even told him I'd asked the mayor over from France. I said I'd be going away and wouldn't be here for the festival, even though I'd arranged it! This villain saw his chance, to get his own back on me and us "ignorant English scum".'

'Who's ignorant?' said the headteacher.

'He did have a point,' said Larry. 'If everyone here thought Kanga Creek was a fine wine from a French chateau!'

* * *

As for the rest of the Festival Week, it all turned out perfectly well, without any further upsets. Harold and the Saxons were able to use the marquee, putting on daily displays of Saxon crafts and cooking, with mock combat (free) at 2.30. Arf had some amazing battles.

As for the fake 'Monsieur Beurre', it turned

out he wasn't a Norman at all, but a Belgian who came from Antwerp. 'But he couldn't have run a restaurant called the *Belgian* Gourmand' said Jim, 'it wouldn't have sounded convincing!'

'Or been so misleading,' said Larry.

Jim offered to do a few stints at the gate, selling the programmes and tickets, with his leg propped up on a chair. So he was the very first person to meet the real Monsieur Beurre. The Mayor came in a big white Citroën with the boot full of camembert cheeses and bottles of Normandy cider.

In fact, the mayor was just in time to see Arf, commanding the Saxons, wipe out a horde of Normans, but he took it all in good spirit.

* * *

That evening, back at Jim Gulliver's house, Larry served up a splendid dinner and everyone drank Norman cider. The Saxons toasted the Normans. The Normans toasted the Saxons. And everyone toasted Jim's plastered leg. Then Monsieur Beurre made a speech, saying how happy he was to be with his English friends, and relieved that the Belgian fraud had been exposed, just in time.

'He came very close, far too close, my friends, to wrecking our new friendship before it had even begun. But he has been thwarted, all thanks to this boy.' He held up his glass. 'To Arf!'

'Arf,' they all shouted. 'Speech, speech, Arf!'

'No, it wasn't just me! It was Bee too.'

'And the Kangarou de la Crique,' Larry said.

'And Hoppa, he caught Patou.'

'Reward,' Jim cried. 'A big bone for the dog and I would like to settle the bill with Slash for his table football.'

'And as for myself,' said the Mayor, 'I want to invite you all for a holiday in St Aubert – including our new Saxon friends who'll be welcome to come and camp and put on displays in our park! With lots more mock combat, eh, Arf?'

'No, I've had enough of mock combat,' said Arf.

'Oh, wow,' said Gloria. 'Really?'

'You just want to run your campsite?' said Vic.

'Not now the festival's over.'

'So what do you want to do?' Harold asked.

'Run a coconut shy?' said Slash.

Arf looked round the happy table, at his family and his friends, and all his Happy Campers. 'I think I might learn to speak French,' he said. 'Properly, like a real Norman.'

About the Author

Philip Wooderson went to school in Kent and studied History at Sussex University. He has worked in a cake mix factory and as a museum researcher, run a restaurant in St Ives, painted lots of pictures and served a short spell in the wine trade before fleeing to Italy.

He has written more than twenty books for children. These include *Arf and the Three Dogs*, *Arf and the Metal Detector*, *Arf and the Greedy Grabber* and Black Cat *Moonmallow Smoothie*. Two of these have been named *Guardian* Book of the Week. Philip has also just completed an adult novel called *Tuscan Madonna*.

About Arf and the Happy Campers:

People often ask me 'Where do you get your ideas from?' Usually I don't have a clue. But for *Arf and the Happy Campers* I'd be happy give a straight answer. My Parents live in Wareham, Dorset. They're very proud of the fact it was founded in Saxon times. To mark it's 1000th birthday the town held a Saxon Festival and people wore Saxon clothes. And at the end of the day we saw a display of 'mock combat'. This was exciting enough, but somehow I couldn't help thinking it would have been MORE exciting if their enemies, the Normans, had joined in the celebrations. Then there could have been a REAL battle!

Another fantastic Black Cat ...

PHILIP WOODERSON
Moonmallow Smoothie

Sam's dad runs an ice cream parlour,
but his business is fast melting
away, thanks to competition from
Karbunkle's Mega Emporiums.

Then, suddenly one night, a
meteorite crashes to Earth in Sam's
garden. It's not just space-rock –
its special properties are perfect for
making ice cream. Soon everyone
wants a taste of Dad's latest invention
called Moonmallow Smoothie.

But Sam's troubles are only
just beginning ...

Another fantastic Black Cat ...

CAROLINE PITCHER
THE GODS ARE WATCHING

Varro is a boy on the run. He's being
chased down the river Nile by a sinister
lord, and he doesn't know why.

Across water and over land,
and even in the deep tunnels beneath
the earth, he has no idea where
his journey will take him,or if
each footstep will bring him closer
to his death. This is an exciting, dramatic
mystery-adventure set in ancient Egypt,
by an award-winning writer.

Black Cats – collect them all!

The Gold-spectre • Elizabeth Arnold

The Ramsbottom Rumble • Georgia Byng

Calamity Kate • Terry Deary

The Custard Kid • Terry Deary

Footsteps in the Fog • Terry Deary

The Ghosts of Batwing Castle • Terry Deary

Ghost Town • Terry Deary

Into the Lion's Den • Terry Deary

The Joke Factory • Terry Deary

The Treasure of Crazy Horse • Terry Deary

The Wishing Well Ghost • Terry Deary

A Witch in Time • Terry Deary

Bryony Bell Tops the Bill • Franzeska G. Ewart

Planimal Magic • Rebecca Lisle

Eyes Wide Open • Jan Mark

The Gods are Watching • Caroline Pitcher

Dear Ms • Joan Poulson

Changing Brooms • Sue Purkiss

Spook School • Sue Purkiss

It's a Tough Life • Jeremy Strong

Big Iggy • Kaye Umansky

Quirky Times at Quagmire Castle • Karen Wallace

Something Slimy on Primrose Drive • Karen Wallace

Drucilla and the Cracked Pot • Lynda Waterhouse

Arf and the Happy Campers • Philip Wooderson

Moonmallow Smoothie • Philip Wooderson